NO LONGER PROPERTY OF
Seattle Public Library

Dear Parents:

Congratulations! Your child is taking the first steps on an exciting journey. The destination? Independent reading!

STEP INTO READING® will help your child get there. The program offers five steps to reading success. Each step includes fun stories and colorful art or photographs. In addition to original fiction and books with favorite characters, there are Step into Reading Non-Fiction Readers, Phonics Readers and Boxed Sets, Sticker Readers, and Comic Readers—a complete literacy program with something to interest every child.

Learning to Read, Step by Step!

Ready to Read   Preschool–Kindergarten
• big type and easy words • rhyme and rhythm • picture clues
For children who know the alphabet and are eager to begin reading.

Reading with Help   Preschool–Grade 1
• basic vocabulary • short sentences • simple stories
For children who recognize familiar words and sound out new words with help.

Reading on Your Own   Grades 1–3
• engaging characters • easy-to-follow plots • popular topics
For children who are ready to read on their own.

Reading Paragraphs   Grades 2–3
• challenging vocabulary • short paragraphs • exciting stories
For newly independent readers who read simple sentences with confidence.

Ready for Chapters   Grades 2–4
• chapters • longer paragraphs • full-color art
For children who want to take the plunge into chapter books but still like colorful pictures.

STEP INTO READING® is designed to give every child a successful reading experience. The grade levels are only guides; children will progress through the steps at their own speed, developing confidence in their reading. The F&P Text Level on the back cover serves as another tool to help you choose the right book for your child.

Remember, a lifetime love of reading starts with a single step!

Copyright © 2017 by Penguin Random House LLC. All rights reserved.
Published in the United States by Random House Children's Books, a division of
Penguin Random House LLC, 1745 Broadway, New York, NY 10019, and in Canada by
Penguin Random House Canada Limited, Toronto. This work is based on *Scuffy the Tugboat* by
Gertrude Crampton, copyright © 1946, 1955, renewed 1973, 1983 by Penguin
Random House LLC. Scuffy the Tugboat is a trademark of Penguin Random House LLC.

Step into Reading, Random House, and the Random House colophon are registered trademarks
of Penguin Random House LLC.

Visit us on the Web!
StepIntoReading.com
randomhousekids.com

Educators and librarians, for a variety of teaching tools, visit us at
RHTeachersLibrarians.com

Library of Congress Cataloging-in-Publication Data
Names: Depken, Kristen L., author. | DiCicco, Sue, illustrator. | Crampton, Gertrude.
Scuffy the tugboat.
Title: Scuffy the tugboat / by Kristen L. Depken ; illustrated by Sue DiCicco.
Description: New York : Random House [2017] | Series: Step into reading.
Step 1, ready to read | "Adapted from the beloved Little Golden Book written by
Gertrude Crampton and illustrated by Tibor Gergely." | Summary: A toy tugboat that
does not want simply to live in a toy store or sail in a bathtub gets more than he
bargained for when he makes a getaway.
Identifiers: LCCN 2015040388 (print) | LCCN 2016020397 (ebook) | ISBN 978-1-101-93929-1 (pb)
| ISBN 978-1-101-93930-7 (glb) | ISBN 978-1-101-93931-4 (ebook)
Subjects: | CYAC: Tugboats—Fiction. | Toys—Fiction. | Adventure and adventurers—Fiction.
Classification: LCC PZ7.D4396 Scu 2017 (print) | LCC PZ7.D4396 (ebook) | DDC
[E]—dc23

Printed in the United States of America
10 9 8 7 6 5 4 3 2 1

This book has been officially leveled by using the F&P Text Level Gradient™ Leveling System.

Random House Children's Books supports the First Amendment and celebrates the right to read.

Scuffy
THE TUGBOAT

Adapted from the beloved Little Golden Book
written by Gertrude Crampton and illustrated by Tibor Gergely

by Kristen L. Depken
illustrated by Sue DiCicco

Random House 🏠 New York

Scuffy is
a little red tugboat.
He does not want
to live in a toy store.
He wants
something bigger!

Scuffy meets a man
with a polka-dot tie.

He takes Scuffy home
to his little boy.

"Sail, little tugboat,"
says the boy.
But Scuffy will not sail
in a bathtub.

A brook!

Now Scuffy will sail.

Scuffy sails away fast.
"This is the life for me!"
he toots.

Scuffy sails
past flowers.

He sails
past woods.

Scuffy sails
past cows.

A cow tries
to drink Scuffy!
That is not fun.

14

Hoot, hoot!

An owl!

Scuffy is scared.

The brook turns
into a river.

Now Scuffy sails
past a small town.

Scuffy sails
past logs.
Ouch!

The river gets bigger and busier.

Scuffy sails
under tall bridges
and past a big town.

He is proud
of his wide river!

The river gets
deeper and deeper.
It moves
faster and faster.

Scuffy moves faster,

too.

A flood!
The river grows
higher and higher.
The people try
to stop it.

Now Scuffy sails

into a big city.

It is busy and noisy!

<u>Toot, toot!</u>

No one hears Scuffy.

He misses the man

with the polka-dot tie.

He misses the boy.

"Oh, oh! The sea!"
cries Scuffy.

Just then,

someone saves Scuffy.

It is the man
with the polka-dot tie!
He takes Scuffy home.

The bathtub!

"This is the life for me!"

Scuffy toots.